Huggles Goes Away

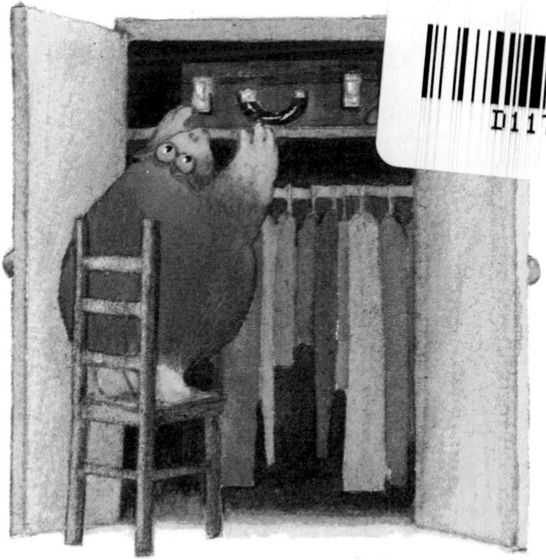

Story by Joy Cowley

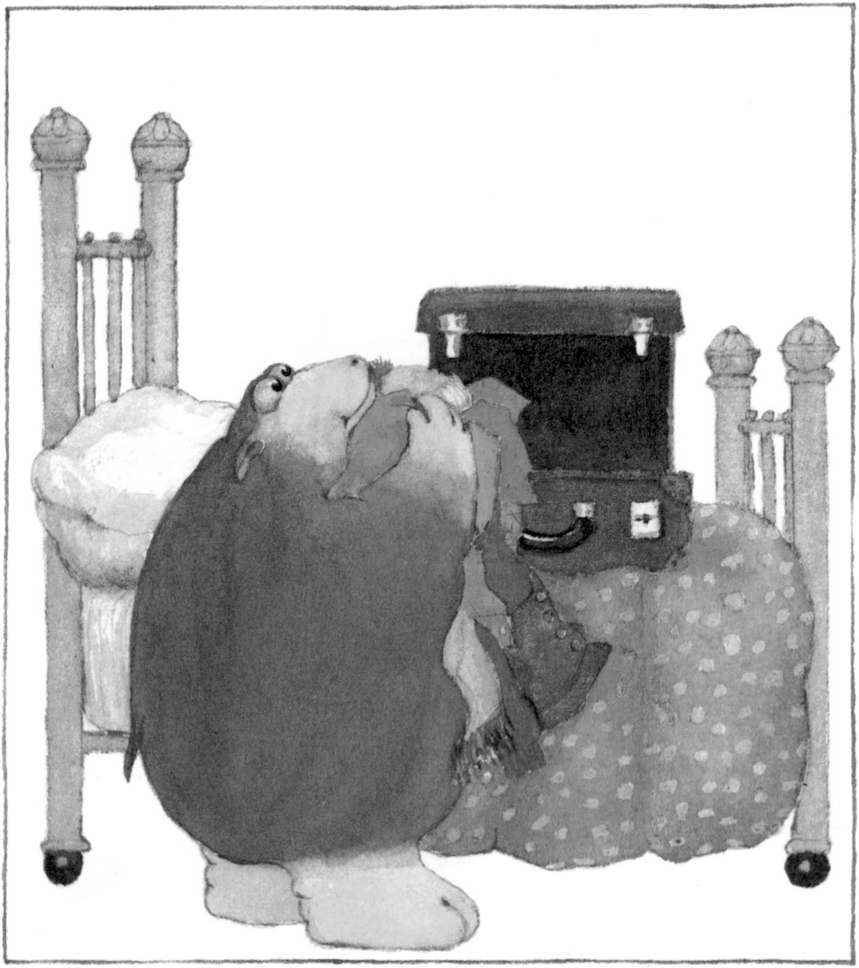

Some clothes,

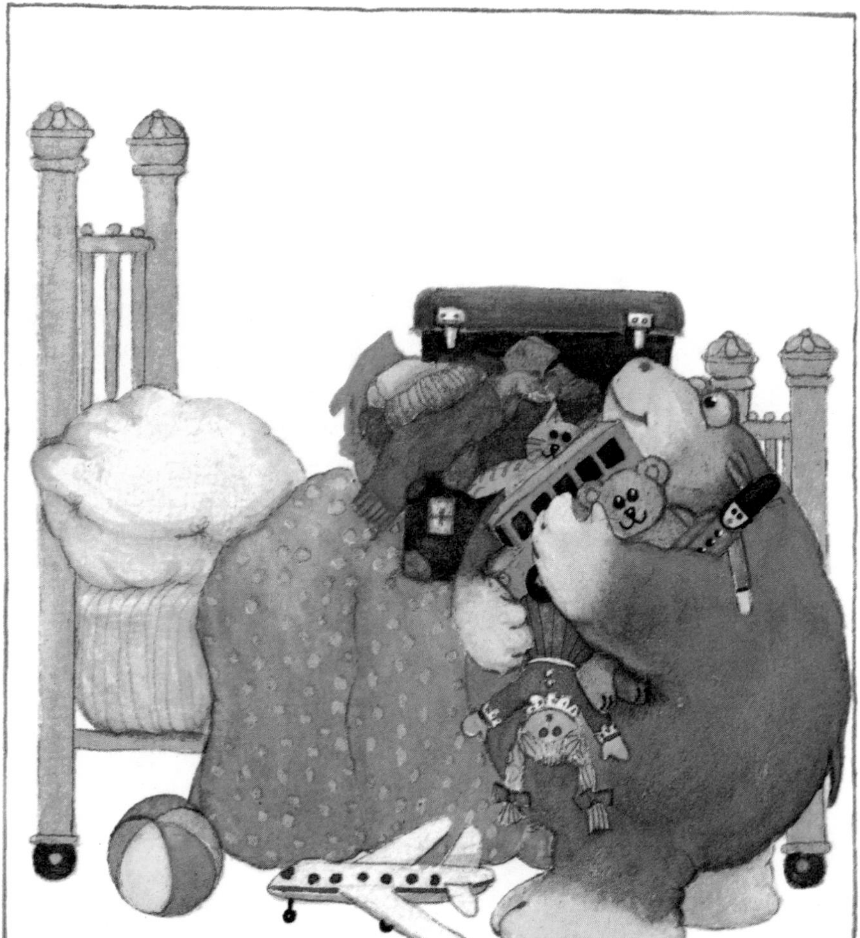

some toys,

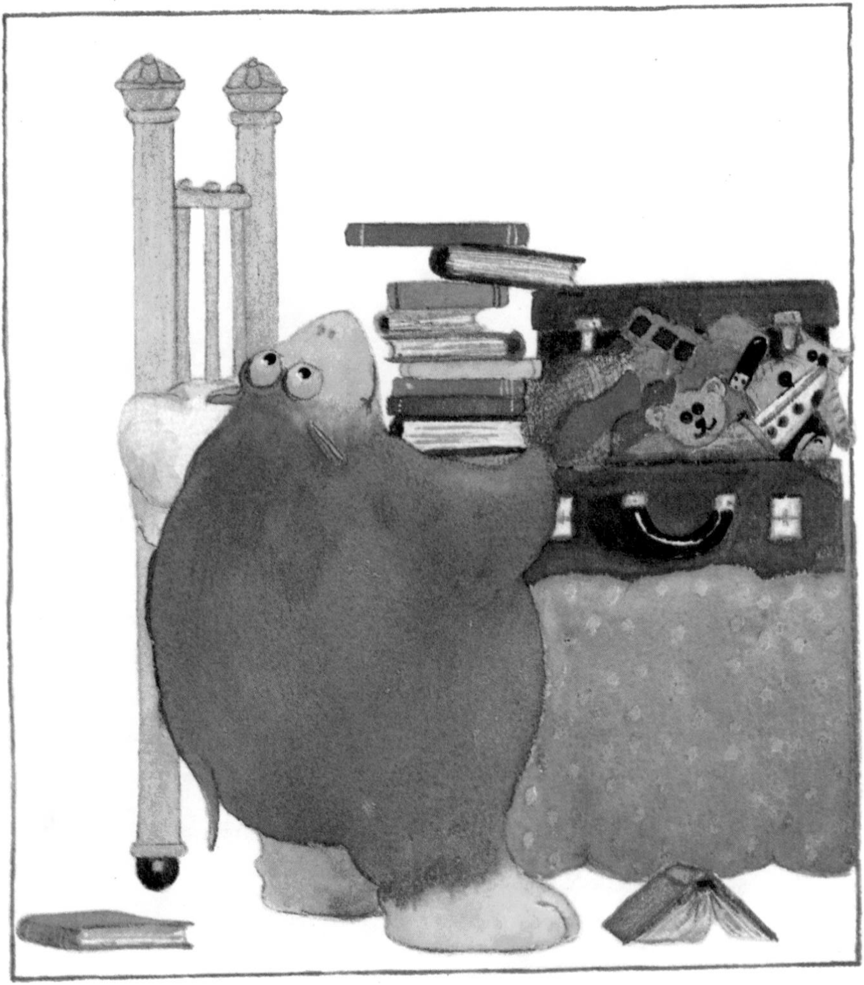

some books,

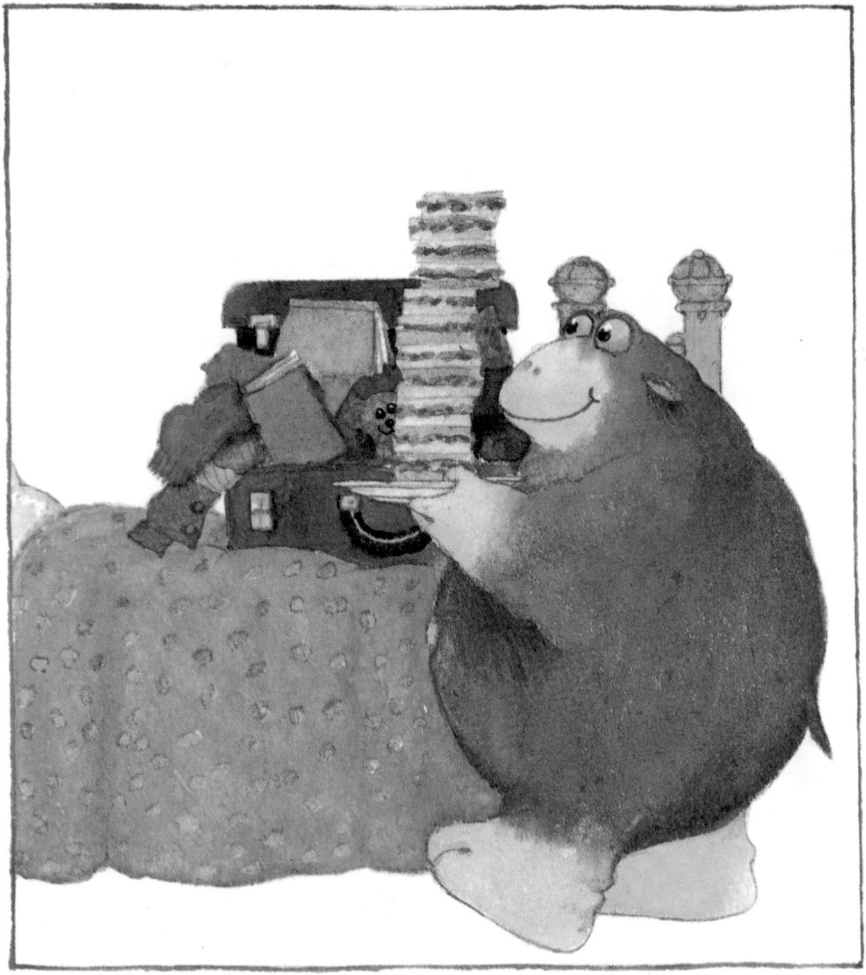

some sandwiches,

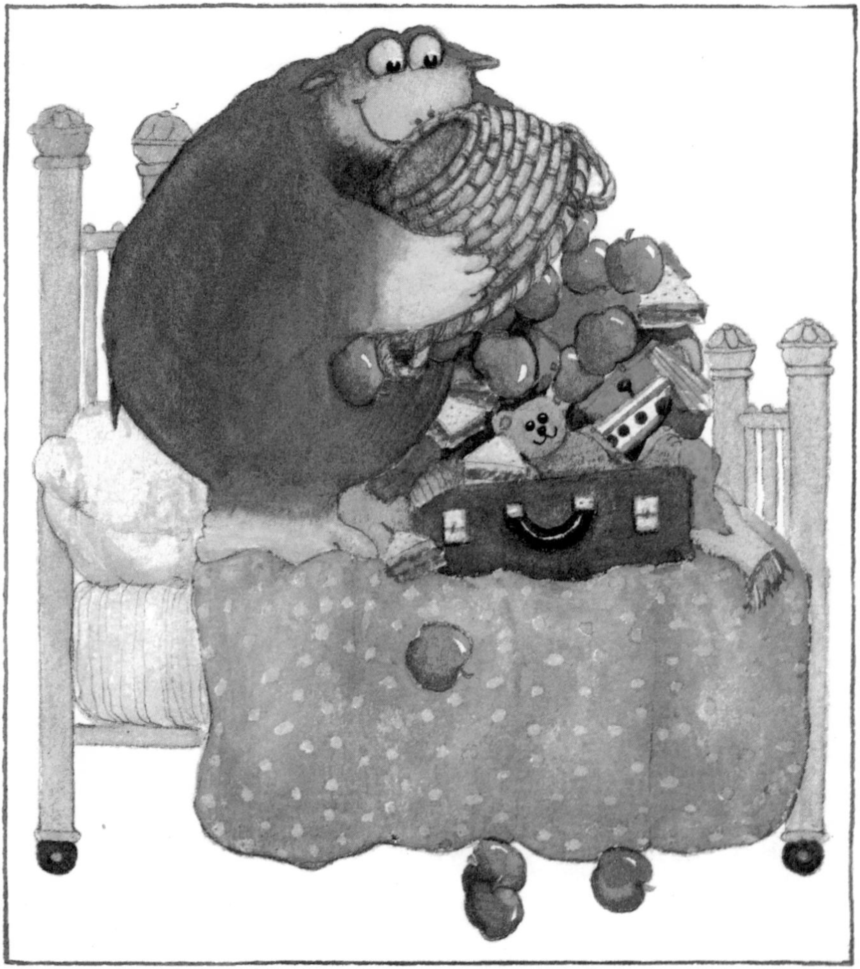

some apples,

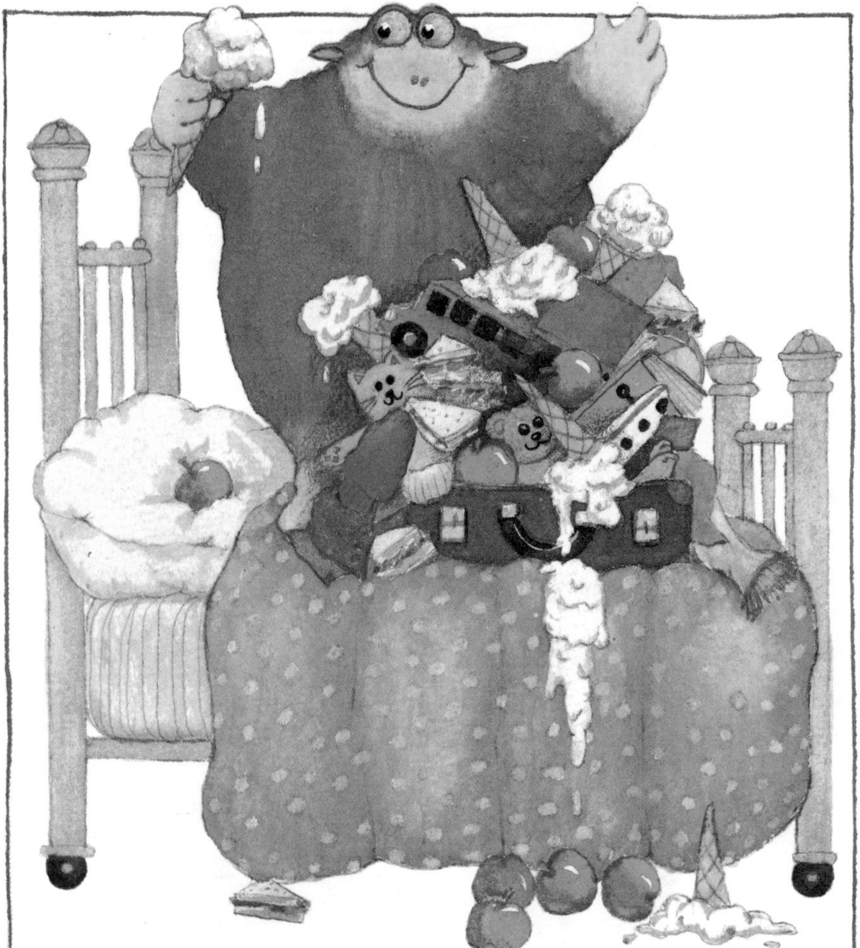

some ice cream.

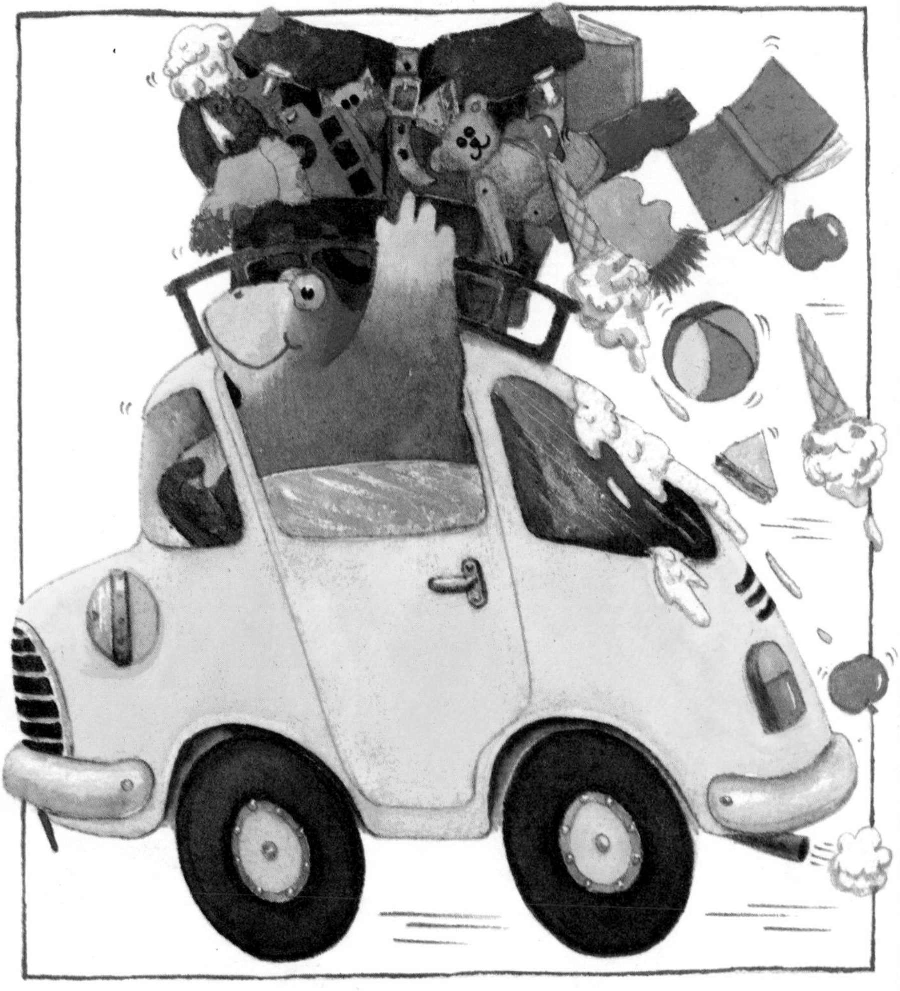

Goodbye!